TRAPPED!

for Emma and the Rayments

TRAPPED!

Mary Small

Illustrated by Trish Hill

sundance

For information regarding permission, write to:
Sundance Publishing
234 Taylor Street
Littleton, MA 01460

Published by
Sundance Publishing
234 Taylor Street
Littleton, MA 01460

First published 1996 by
Addison Wesley Longman Australia Pty Limited
95 Coventry Street
South Melbourne 3205 Australia
Exclusive United States Distribution: Sundance Publishing

ISBN 0-7608-0773-6

It's hot in the classroom. *Stinking* hot.
I look around. Everyone's writing except me.
Don't they *feel* the heat?

5

Here I am sweating like a pig with Smart Alec right beside me, his nose almost touching the table and his arm curled around the paper so that I can't see his work.

I wouldn't want to copy from him. I can't be bothered, and I'm not a cheat.

Alec really annoys me and the rest of our class. His real name's Dwayne, but I reckon his mother got it wrong. He's Alec to us.

Whenever Miss Fizzwick, our teacher, asks a question, up shoots his hand, waving wildly like a helicopter rotor blade. He's such a know-it-all.

This classroom's *so* hot I shall die, and here's
Fizzwick coming straight for me!

"What's the problem, Julian?" she says,
then stares in amazement at my blank sheet
of paper.

She looks at her watch.

"Ten minutes of the hour gone already.
You'd better hurry up and get started."

"With what?"

"You know perfectly well," she whispers,
so as not to disturb the others.

13

"I can't write stories. I don't have any ideas," I remind her.

Fizzwick pokes her finger at the blank paper accusingly. "Julian," she says, "if writing a story is really that difficult for you, just try to make some sort of an effort. It's a shame you got nothing out of Trudi Trubshaw's visit."

I watch Fizzwick's backview as she continues her prowl around the classroom. Veronica Fizzwick. What a name! It's unreal!

I reckon Trudi Trubshaw was a bit unreal, too.
She was the "real live famous author" who came
to our school for Book Week. So this week we
have to write stories. I'm not quite sure what we
expected a "real live famous author" to look like.
Fizzwick was shocked when Gordon Parsons
asked her how old she was.

16

"I'm a little bit older than Bugs Bunny," she replied. Immediately, we all began discussing among ourselves Bugs Bunny's age.

"Are you seventy?" I asked.

Trudi Trubshaw laughed but Fizzwick went "Tsk. Tsk."

"I'm not quite that old," said Trudi Trubshaw. "But age has nothing to do with writing books." I suppose that's true.

We had a good time with Trudi Trubshaw. She made us laugh, and it was heaps better than doing boring classwork. Fizzwick is always on us about our spelling, but Trudi Trubshaw said spelling wasn't as important as story and style.

"A publisher will be impressed if you have a good story to tell and it's well-written," she told us. "There shouldn't be any problem finding story ideas. Just keep a check on what happens around you. And use your imagination."

The trouble is I don't have any imagination.
And when Trudi Trubshaw told us how much
money she had made from writing books,
I decided I didn't want to be an author.
I'm going to be a Rollerblade™ champ instead.

I look around the classroom again. Scribble.
Scribble. Scribble. I suppose they've all got
mind-boggling stories.

Smart Alec must be writing a new version of the Bible. I nudge his elbow so his pen slips. He looks up angrily.

"Nerd!" he hisses.

"Your hand should be up on the ceiling. We could use it for a fan!" I retort.

Rick and Simon, sitting opposite, grin and roll their eyes.

My watch tells me time's dragging. Uh! Oh! Fizzwick's steely eyes are on me so I put my nose down and my arm around the page like Alec and start scribbling. Just lines going round and round and round and round . . .

Z z z z z z z.

I look up. There's a fly in the classroom.
A really big humdinger of a blowfly.
It's come through the open window.
                    Z z z z z.

It zooms towards our table and circles just like
my scribbling, round and round and round.

Then it takes off after Fizzbuzz . . .
I mean Fizzwick!

Fizzzz! I've got it! I'll write a story about Fizzwick the blowfly! Then what? Eliminate her! Splat!

I'm good at drawing so I carefully draw the fly and its segmented eyes.

"Fizzzz!" I say out loud and bang my hand down hard on the picture. Splat!

"Stop it!" growls Alec, glaring at me.

Rick and Simon make more faces and laugh.

I've got a better idea! So brilliant that I'm amazed when my arm is pulled away from the table and there's Fizzwick again.

"This looks more industrious, Julian," she says, and stares at the drawing I've done of the fly and the scribbled notes written beside it. "An excellent drawing. Is this your main character? A fly?"

"Yes, Miss Fizzwick. It's a blowfly."

"What's this word 'Fizzzz' mean?"
"The special noise a blowfly makes,
Miss Fizzwick."

"And the rest of these notes you've jotted down?
Venus Flytrap, Snap. Stuck inside. History?"

"A Venus Flytrap is a carnivorous plant,"
I tell her. "They catch insects. They're really
amazing, Miss Fizzwick."

"Tell me more, Julian."

"When a fly lands on the open leaves, it triggers tiny little hairs that snap the leaves shut like jaws. The fly is trapped inside like a prisoner. It struggles madly, but the more it struggles the tighter the jaws clamp. So the fly slowly dies as the plant sucks out its juices."

"It sounds perfectly horrible," says Miss
Fizzwick. "Like a 'blood and guts' story."

And remember Trudi Trubshaw said that 'blood and guts' was a lazy way of getting out of really thinking about a story."

33

"Carnivorous plants are really amazing, Miss Fizzwick," I continue. But she's no longer interested, as Smart Alec wants her attention.

"You've precisely thirty-five minutes left," she warns me. "If you are going to persist in writing a story about a fly being caught in a flytrap then change your story to the first person."

"First person. What's that?"

"You know perfectly well what the first person means. This flytrap has snapped shut on you!"

"Then that's simple. I'll be history!"

"Well then, write how you managed to be small enough to get trapped and how you feel about the situation."

"Trapped!" I reply with a smile.

Miss Fizzwick ignores me.

The blowfly is nowhere to be seen. It must have flown out of the window. I feel grateful because it's given me the idea for my story.

I could tell Fizzwick how Mom hates Dad's carnivorous plants being in the den.
And that she says they're disgusting but that Dad always points out that there aren't any flies. I reckon it's truly amazing how a plant can trap and eat an insect.

It's a shame Fizzwick's not into nature.
I could tell the class about all sorts of
carnivorous plants.

There are flytraps that attract insects
with a sweet-smelling nectar. And
Sticky Sundews and Pitcher Plants
where insects crawl inside and slide
down to their doom.

Trust Fizzwick to stick me into the flytrap instead of her. She knows I hate school, and she always accuses me of being an attention-seeker. I can't help it if I'm dumb.

I start drawing again, this time a Bombardier Beetle. Bombardier Beetles shoot foul-smelling boiling chemicals from their abdomens at their enemies.

If I were a Bombardier Beetle, I could zap Miss Fizzwick. If I were a humungous Bombardier Beetle, I could eliminate the school. Wow!

I can't help admiring the beetle I've drawn. Maybe, one day, I could become a rich and famous illustrator. Better than an author.

"Julian Sproggle!" Fizzwick is back again. She picks up my paper. "What *is* this drawing?"

"A Bombardier Beetle, Miss Fizzwick. All these dots are the boiling chemicals coming out of its abdomen."

"I thought I'd left you struggling for your life inside the Venus Flytrap?"

"You did, but I can't think of how I became so small!"

Miss Fizzwick stands up straight and tall and calls the class to attention. "Pens down, please, just for a minute. Julian needs our help." Everyone is grinning at me.

Miss Fizzwick tells them my idea. I was really pleased to see that Smart Alec obviously didn't know anything about Venus Flytraps although he pretended that he did.

"Carnivorous means meat-eater," he tells everyone.

"Correct," says Miss Fizzwick.

"Like a lion!" says Simon, opposite.

"Precisely," says Miss Fizzwick, "except Julian is stuck in a meat-eating plant and is trying to escape."

I pull Miss Fizzwick's arm. "How did I get there in the first place?" I whisper. "I'd have to be tiny."

"Right, everyone," says Miss Fizzwick. "Julian needs to know how to become tiny."

Smart Alec's hand is up and waving like a helicopter rotor blade again. "It could be a dream," he says.

"Dreams are an easy way out," says Miss Fizzwick. "I know it's too hot to think in here, but let's try for some other ideas."

"You could drink something that makes you shrink," says Anita.

"Or walk through a door and find yourself small," says Ben.

Tyson, big bully-boy sitting at the table behind me, sticks his fingers into my back.

"Zap! I've zapped you small!" he says.

"Excellent," says Miss Fizzwick. "Julian is now small, having been zapped by Tyson and then trapped in a meat-eating plant. Everyone, continue writing while I help Julian think of a way to save himself."

"I must've been stupid to have got caught in the first place," I remark.

"Perhaps you weren't concentrating on where you were going."

"Something like that. Dad always says I don't concentrate."

I put my pen down and look at Miss Fizzwick hopelessly. "I'm doomed to die! I deserve it!" I tell her.

"Nonsense!" says Miss Fizzwick. "We can't let that happen. I, for one, would miss you."

I stare at Miss Fizzwick. I think she really means it!

Miss Fizzwick puts the pen back in my hand. "Now," she says "put your brain into gear and use your imagination. You've twenty minutes left!" she says to everyone.

Twenty minutes! The time is really flying.

I suppose I could use a sword or a laser gun, but the leaves of the Venus Flytrap are clamped so tight I can't move. It's even difficult to breathe. And while I struggle desperately to get out, the juices are already gurgling. It's no good. I shout "Help!" but nobody hears.

The juices are up to my knees now. Mom will be really mad when she finds my new sneakers ruined. That's all anybody will find ... my sneakers, clothes, teeth, and bones! Gurgle, Gurgle, Gurgle. The noise is deafening.

"Help!" I scream, waving my hands in the air.

"Help! Miss Fizzwick! Help!"
Everyone looks up in astonishment, and Fizzwick comes running.

"I told you I'm history!" I gasp, and collapse in a heap on the desk.

Laughter ripples round the classroom. Miss Fizzwick pulls me firmly up by the shoulder and she's smiling too. "Julian Sproggle. You'd make a good clown!" she says.

Just then somebody burps from way down the other end of the room. More laughter, but Miss Fizzwick pretends not to hear.

"Right," she says. "Those of you who have finished can bring their work to my desk."

57

Burp! That's it! If I could get the Flytrap to burp, I could escape! I write BURP (with a large exclamation mark beside it) so I don't forget. Maybe I'm wearing a suit of armor and the plant can't digest me. So it burps. Or perhaps I could tickle it inside if I had a feather.

Better still, I smell! My feet are really smelly...
not only my feet but all of me. Mom always says
my feet and sneakers are a walking gas attack. I
smell so bad the plant can't stand it. Hey presto,
it burps and I fly out with all the juices.

I'm so pleased with myself that I burp on purpose, so loud that everyone hears. The class collapses. I burp again.

'Julian Sproggle, stand up!" Miss Fizzwick orders.

I stand with pride. Like Alec I wave my arms in the air like the rotor blades of a helicopter.

"I know the answer!" I shout. "The Venus Flytrap hates smelly me so it burped and spat me out!"

"Cool! Really cool!" shouts everyone.

The recess bell goes. There's an immediate scraping of chairs and a rush like the wind for the door. Finished and unfinished stories are piled on Miss Fizzwick's desk.

When everyone's gone, she stares at me still sitting in my place.

"Julian," she says, "it's recess."

"I know," I say, "but I've got to finish this story."

"I don't believe it," she says and walks out of the classroom.

I keep writing. The spelling's not too good, but I reckon Trudi Trubshaw would be proud of me. Maybe I could show her my story, and she could tell me where to find a publisher.

BOOK OF THE YEAR

Perhaps, after all, I could become a rich and famous author!